Gertrude always loved trolling the trolls. In the good old days through editorials in the papers. In recent years through the comments sections on online articles.

Nothing beats the pleasure of watching the bigots and jerks of the net scramble to agree with Gertrude's fake personas and shoot themselves in the foot as they invariably show their true colors or contradict themselves.

With her granddaughter's invaluable help on navigating the dangers of the net, Gertude fights the battles of those who are not as lucky, right from her late husband's too-large office chair.

R.W. WALLACE

Author of the Ghost Detective Series

GERTRUDE
and the
TROJAN HORSE
A Geriatric Short Story

Gertrude and the Trojan Horse

by R.W. Wallace

Copyright © 2019 by R.W. Wallace

Copy editing by Jinxie Gervasio

Illustration by Maxtrella

Cover by the author

All characters and events in this book, other than those clearly in the public domain, are fictitious and any resemblance to real persons, living or dead, is purely coincidental.

All rights reserved. No part of this publication may be reproduced, distributed, or transmitted in any form or by any means, including photocopying, recording, or other electronic or mechanical methods, without the prior written permission of the publisher, except in the case of brief quotations embodied in critical reviews and certain other noncommercial uses permitted by copyright law. For permission requests, write to the publisher, addressed "Attention: Permissions Coordinator," at the address below.

www.rwwallace.com

ISBN: [979-10-95707-31-8]

Main category—Fiction
Other category—Mystery

First Edition

Also by R.W. Wallace

Mystery

The Tolosa Mystery Series
The Red Brick Haze (free)
The Red Brick Cellars
The Red Brick Basilica

Ghost Detective Shorts (coming soon)
Just Desserts
Lost Friends
Family Bonds
Till Death
Common Ground

Short Stories
Hidden Horrors
Critters
Gertrude and the Trojan Horse
First Impressions
Let Them Eat Cake
Out of Sight
Two's Company

Science Fiction (short stories)
The Vanguard
Quarantine (Lollapalooza)
Common Enemies (Lollapalooza)

Adventure (short stories)
Size Matters

Urban Fantasy (short stories)
Unexpected Consequences

GERTRUDE

AND THE

TROJAN HORSE

Gertrude pushed her glasses up her nose, to better see the screen in front of her. She stretched her neck and pursed her lips, tilting her head back so the text she wanted to read was aligned with the best part of her lenses.

Make sure the page is secure, the text read, *i.e. that the URL starts with "https." If it's not, quit the page and call me.*

Gertrude pressed the Alt and Tab buttons on her laptop to display the webpage she was visiting. Https present. Okay, then.

Shifting in her seat, making the massive chair creak under her light weight, Gertrude nodded in satisfaction. This was such *fun*. The internet hadn't been available when Robert was alive. They'd only had TV and newspapers to get information, and no way of participating—except by sending in pieces to certain columns inviting readers to offer their two cents.

Gertrude gave a contented sigh at the memory of Robert trolling the recently elected mayor by sending in a piece that *appeared* to support him, at least to someone who didn't have the slightest grasp on sarcasm. Having read the column in question for years, Gertrude and Robert were well aware of this particular editor's shortcomings.

That particular piece unfortunately marked the end of that loophole, since the editor got fired for printing something putting the mayor in such bad light. The replacement understood sarcasm all too well.

Gertrude continued enjoying her fun over the years since Robert passed, but she never managed to come up with quite the same level of trolling as they'd done as a team. You need one person to come up with the idea, then the other to grab it and run for the hills. Metaphorically speaking, of course. Gertrude hadn't run in decades.

The last point on her list read, *You can accept messages for cookies, and for Privacy Settings. If the website wants to know your location, refuse.*

Gertrude ran her tongue along her upper dentures as she read the headline of the top story. She didn't really need to use her granddaughter's checklist to read the news, but her mind wasn't what it used to be and she didn't want to take any chances. Also, she enjoyed the reminder of her sweet little girl who helped her out and knew so much about all this modern technology.

Not that Gertrude was too shabby, herself. She moved the wireless mouse and clicked on the first article. Several pages of text and accompanying photos appeared. Magic.

And at the bottom, the real gold: the comments.

Depending on the website, people were more or less restrained in what they wrote. If you had to sign your comment and give your whole name, or at least sign in with your Facebook account, people stayed somewhat civil. Somewhat.

But on the sites where you could comment anonymously, or with any name you could come up with? People really let loose.

Just last week, on this very website, she'd trolled a bigot who wrote over ten paragraphs arguing why women should be the ones to stay at home with the kids, and cook, and do laundry, and…you get the picture. Gertrude was seventy-five years old, and even she hadn't had to suffer through a marriage like that. She *had* done the laundry—but not the cooking.

Which meant she'd been eating junk food and whatever her family prepared for her for fifteen years, but that was a different topic entirely.

Anyway, the bigot had it coming.

Taking her time, typing one letter at a time, using only her right hand index finger, Gertrude posted a comment as "P. Petit," agreeing to absolutely everything the idiot said. And adding to it. The women should only be allowed cell phones if their husbands allowed it. They could only leave the house if it had first been authorized by the husband. They should have an allowance of no more than fifty euros a week—to make sure they don't spend all day shopping.

He'd taken the bait, of course. Went on a new rant, taking things even further.

One more comment from Gertrude, and his final reply was enough to bring hundreds of people in to tell him what an idiot he was, to get banned from the website, and to create a meme that was still doing its rounds on Twitter and Reddit. Seemed like he'd used his real name, so the question now was whether or not he'd keep his job.

Today's article on Trump just didn't catch Gertrude's interest. Even the comments were faded and lacking inspiration. You call a guy an idiot enough times, and you actually get tired of it.

Gertrude scanned the other articles, her gnarly finger moving smoothly over the wheel allowing to scroll down the page. Wonderful stuff. No ink on her fingers, no cramps in her arms from holding up the large pages.

Elderly couple loses life savings to scam artists. Frowning, Gertrude clicked on the article.

A couple in their eighties were scammed out of the majority of their savings by a young man coming to their home, pretending to install fiber connection in their house—for free. Of course, they did no such thing, but used a USB drive to install a Trojan horse on the couple's computer, and over the next couple of weeks, used the access this gained them to empty out the savings accounts.

Gertrude opened the files her granddaughter had prepared for her. *A Trojan horse is like opening the back door to your house. It allows others to come into and control your computer from afar. Usually comes through clicking on links, opening attached files, or from an unknown USB drive.*

Right. Gertrude remembered now. Although the idea of a bunch of hunky Greek men jumping out of her computer sounded mighty fine, Trojan horses were a big no no.

The article was already a couple of days old, so the comments were plentiful. Gertrude took her time and read them all.

Some bemoaned how difficult it was for the older generation to understand all the high tech stuff of today, and no wonder if the scammers went after them. Some railed at the scammers for attacking the most vulnerable. Some accused the banks of not having sufficiently secured their websites to protect against this type of attack. This created a whole thread of its own, as some Peter guy, who clearly knew his stuff, explained all the intricacies of what the banks put in place, but if the computer was accessed remotely while a person was accessing his accounts, even the brightest program couldn't detect it. The less techy commenters accused him of being a pompous ass.

Usually, Gertrude would have found this highly amusing. But she agreed too much with the fact that it was difficult for most people of her generation to do everything on their computers instead of in person. Everybody didn't have a granddaughter with an engineering degree in computers—actually, it was a different word, but Gertrude's mind always translated it into "computers." That was the gist of it, anyway.

One profile had left three different comments, each one saying that if they didn't know how to use the tools, they shouldn't. If they left themselves open to attack, they deserved being robbed. Would anyone bemoan someone for getting robbed if they left their front door open every time they left the house?

The little picture going with the account making the comment—the avatar—looked familiar. Gertrude used her notes to figure out how to zoom in. It was some sort of rat or mouse, dressed up as Robin Hood.

Gertrude had seen this avatar before. It was used frequently on a forum she sometimes clicked around on when she was bored, one dedicated to life hacks. For most users, this meant sharing tips on how to reuse old sheets, or get wine stains out of shirts, but for some—and Rat Robin Hood was one of these—it meant finding loopholes to earn a quick buck without actually working. Gertrude had tried baiting the man several times, but he never took the bait.

Gertrude checked her notes, then opened her calendar. Superposed with her own—mostly empty, for obvious reasons—was her granddaughter's schedule. She had tomorrow off.

Gertrude grinned at the screen. She was going to have some fun, but this would take an accomplice.

ভ

"Are you sure about this, Mamie?" Céline, the granddaughter, sat in front of Gertrude's computer, her fingers poised over the keyboard, ready to do business. Still, she hesitated. "I don't like you putting yourself in danger like this." Her green eyes pleaded with Gertrude, a tiny worry line appearing between her eyebrows.

"I'll be fine," Gertrude said. She was in her usual seat, in Robert's old office chair, the old thing swallowing her up, making her look even more small and frail than she actually was. Gertrude loved this chair, with its worn leather and squeaky hinges. It smelled like Robert, and engulfed her, just like he had done.

Gertrude patted Céline's hand. "We do everything like we've planned, and I won't be in any physical danger. I trust you."

Céline looked like she wanted to argue, but after a glimpse at her grandmother's face, she gave up. She knew her well enough to realize when there was no point in trying to change her mind.

"Fine," she finally conceded with a sigh. "But don't say I didn't warn you."

She started typing.

ఎ

A FEW DAYS later, Gertrude was composing a comment to a young girl who felt left out because all her friends had Gucci handbags and she didn't, when the doorbell rang.

Gertrude never had unexpected visitors. She quickly shut down her browser window and clicked on the big green button in the middle of her desktop that Céline had helpfully labeled "click here!"

A window opened, then closed again. The green button disappeared.

Well. Guess she was ready.

The doorbell rang again. Gertrude called out, "Just a minute!" before hurrying to the bathroom. She removed her dentures and dropped them in a glass of water. The glass she brought with her back to the living room, where she set it up in plain sight, right next to the computer.

Satisfied with the set-up, Gertrude shuffled to the front door, and opened it with a wide, toothless grin.

"Morning, Ma'am." The young man on her doorstep didn't look like he could be a day over twelve—which probably meant he was in his early twenties. "I'm here to fix your phone issue?" He had a pretty enough face, if you liked 'em tall and lanky, but his eyebrows arched high on his forehead and his blue eyes were rather big, which gave the impression of him being perpetually surprised. Finishing statements like they were questions didn't help the issue.

"Phone issue?" Gertrude practically spat on the man. Pronunciation was quite impossible with only bottom teeth. And saliva was something to be shared.

"I got a call saying that your land line ain't working? I'm here to fix it."

Gertrude adopted a look of confusion, but inside she was jumping with glee. It worked!

After Céline had done her thing, Gertrude composed a question on the life hack forum. She'd asked what an old lady was to do when she kept calling the phone company to come fix her land line, but nobody ever showed. She really needed that phone, because she had to call the bank and ask them how on earth she was supposed to use their website to send money to her grandchildren.

The saddest part of the whole thing was that it worked because it was exactly the type of question most of Gertrude's generation asked.

Gertrude flashed the surprised-looking boy her gums and lower teeth, and bit back a laugh when he fought not to wince. "Finally!" she said—or rather "phinally"—and opened the door wide to let him in. "I've been calling for help for weeks, and nobody ever wants to help an old lady." At least that's what she tried to say but talking without teeth was torture—for the both of them.

As she led the young man into her living room, Gertrude picked up her dentures from the glass of water and held them up to show to her visitor. "Juths going to fof 'em back in." She proceeded to pull the oral adhesive out of the pocket of her jeans, spread it out on the false gums, and shoved the dentures back in place in her mouth.

"There," she said and smacked her lips in satisfaction. "Much better."

The young man looked suitably icked out. With those eyebrows, he really could have made a fortune playing in horror movies, because his current expression made Gertrude want to turn around to see what the monster behind her might be.

Gertrude pointed to the kitchen. "The phone is right in here, young man."

"Uh…actually, I only need to see your computer?" He gulped and surreptitiously dried his palms on his thighs.

"But my problem is with my phone, not my computer." Gertrude shuffled over to her chair, and sank into its leathery depths, despite it being in front of the computer and not in the kitchen. She might be ready to open her house to the man to troll him, but her chair was sacred. His scrawny little arse wasn't getting anywhere near it.

"Ah, but you see, it's all linked, right?" He seemed to be getting over the whole toothless old lady thing and was moving back to a script he knew well. "You're paying your internet through your phone provider, right? If you don't have internet, you don't have a phone? It's all linked. I just want to check that everything's peachy on your computer. That's where the problems usually come from?"

"I don't really understand any of this stuff," Gertrude said as she made her best lost-old-lady face. "I trust you." On the inside, she chortled. As if she'd trust a twelve-year-old with her computer. Might as well trust Trump with the nuclear codes. Ha. Ha.

Dammit, that one still hurt.

With a victorious smile, the young man sat down in front of the computer. He touched the touchpad, making the login screen appear.

"What's your password?" He had a block of yellow Post-it notes ready, and took one of Gertrude's pens, ready to write.

Gertrude popped out of her chair. Now that the youngster was seated in the old fold-down chair in front of the computer, she could risk vacating her seat. "Would you like some coffee? And I have pie!"

"Uh." He stayed crouched over the Post-it, as if afraid of missing the password as it flew past. "Just your password, please?"

"You *must* have some coffee and pie." Gertrude set two cups on the kitchen table and poured the coffee that had been brewing since early that morning. "I hardly ever have any visitors. Sometimes I think that if I dropped dead, nobody would notice until the neighbors wondered about the smell."

The boy didn't know what to say to this. Youngsters were usually quite ill at ease talking about old age and death, since it was such a foreign concept to them. "Your pass—"

"So you simply *have* to taste my pie," Gertrude continued. "Personally, I find it delicious, but I can't eat it because my doctor's told me to stop eating sugar." She dropped two sugar cubes in each of the coffees, and briskly stirred them with a spoon.

She grabbed the plate that had stood ready on her counter for two days—oh, yes, this pie was perfection—and put it on top of the Post-its. "Eat," she said.

The young man looked up at her, irritation and indecisiveness written on his smooth features. If he was looking for guile, he wouldn't find it; Gertrude was a pro. Also, if anything did show, this youngster wouldn't recognize it. There were *some* advantages to being covered in wrinkles.

"Eat," Gertrude repeated.

"I just need—"

"Eat. You're only skin and bones. Make an old lady happy and eat the pie."

He might be stealing money from the elderly today, but somewhere in his past, parents had given the boy a proper upbringing. He set down his pen and accepted the pie. It wasn't very big, but it was *solid*. The crust was perfect, nicely brown on top and crisp to the touch. Inside, Gertrude had mixed up every fiber-rich fruit she could put her hands on, added in some laxative from the pharmacy, and filled up with spices like cinnamon and cardamom, just to make sure.

"Uh." The boy seemed to have trouble chewing but managed to force down the first bite. "I don't—"

"I do hope you like it," Gertrude said as she leaned closer. "I made that especially for you. Do you not like dried fruit? Or is it the cinnamon? Perhaps if I just remove—" She made as if to shove her finger into the pie.

"It's great," he said quickly, and moved the plate out of Gertrude's reach. He shoved a large piece into his mouth, chewed—clearly without tasting it—and swallowed. Fifteen seconds later, the pie was gone.

Gulping, he eyed the two cups of coffee on the kitchen counter. "Could I...you mentioned coffee?" As he caught a gastric reflux, he added, "I really need your password if you want me to help you?"

Gertrude shuffled toward the kitchen, her slippers making their usual swish, swish. She hadn't bothered to really lift her feet in a few years. Worked just as well this way.

"The password's my birthday," she said. "Twelve, ten, nineteen eleven."

"Thank you." The young boy noted the numbers on his post-it, then tapped the code to log onto the computer.

Really? He believed she was over a hundred years old? Gertrude shook her head. The kids today…

He arrived on a desktop that he should have found suspiciously empty, but the boy just brought a USB drive out of his little bag and inserted it into one of the computer's slots.

This was Gertrude's signal. With both coffees in hand, she leaned forward, as if to see better what was going on. "What is that for?" she asked.

"It's nothing, really. I just—" He broke off in a scream.

Gertrude had successfully upended both coffees down his neck and on his lap—she hadn't even spilled a single drop on the computer!

Eyebrows literally disappearing into his ruffled hair, mouth open in a silent scream, the boy tore at his clothes.

Really, that was a bit of an over-reaction, wasn't it? The coffee was warm, but far from boiling... At worst, he'd have some reddened skin.

Still, the plan was working perfectly. Pushing the chair back, the youngster pulled his t-shirt over his head, and his cargo shorts quickly followed suit. He stood before Gertrude in nothing but a pair of Superman boxers, panting heavily with wild eyes that seemed about ready to pop out of his little head.

On the screen behind him, a window popped open, then closed again immediately.

"What'd you that for?" The poor boy was shivering, coffee trickling down his skinny torso and his surprisingly hairy legs.

Gertrude put her hands on her cheeks. "I'm so terribly sorry. I completely forgot I had those cups in my hands! Here, let me make it up to you." She pulled open the closet behind her, praying the boy wouldn't find it suspicious that she kept her dead husband's clothes in a closet in the middle of the living room. "You can borrow something to wear. Let me just see if I can find something your size."

She couldn't, of course. Robert had been a first liner rugby player, with shoulders so wide Gertrude had never managed to touch her hands when holding him, and legs so long he'd never been able to travel economy class on an airplane.

Her little scammer didn't know this, though. He stood, patiently waiting, while Gertrude emptied the entire closet, holding up shirts and shorts, sweaters and pants, only to discard them.

In the end, he lost patience. "I'll just wear this," he said, and pulled the latest t-shirt from the growing pile and throwing it on.

He looked ridiculous, but was clearly beyond caring, as he sat back down in front of the computer.

"What's this?" he asked.

On the screen, a Greek hunk of meat wearing a himation, traipsed across the screen.

Gertrude smiled so hard her dentures almost fell out. Céline had left her a little present. "It's a Trojan," she replied.

"What?" His head whipped to stare at Gertrude. "That's not what a Trojan is."

"Yes, it is," she replied, giggling. "A Trojan is a Greek guy. They liked fighting. Hence all the muscles." She waggled her eyebrows.

Which apparently didn't sit too well with the young man, who turned back to the computer to retrieve his USB drive. "I need to get going now, Ma'am." He stood and put his USB drive back in his bag.

"Is the phone working?" Gertrude asked.

"Sorry, I couldn't find anything." He shrugged and took a step toward the door.

"But you haven't even looked at the phone." If he had, he would have seen that it was in perfect working order.

"I don't know, Ma'am. My job is just to look at the computer. If the problem's with the phone, one of my colleagues will have to look at it?" He put a hand on his abdomen and took a step toward the door.

Gertrude moved to intercept him—the fact that she managed to do so was a testament to how well her pie was working. "There was never a problem with my computer," she said, pretending to be confused. "My problem's with my phone. Why did they send you?"

The youngster shrugged, eying the distance to the door, and the old lady blocking his way. He flinched and drew a breath, bending a little at the waist.

"I need to call my bank," Gertrude said, getting into the young man's face. "I can't do that without a phone."

"Fine," he whispered. "Where's the god-damned phone?"

"Right here." Gertrude moved some papers from her desk and pulled out a wireless phone that had been the latest hype when she bought it some twenty years ago.

The youngster took it. He didn't even pretend to be able to stand up straight anymore. He bent over with one hand on his knee as he pressed several buttons on the phone.

"The battery's dead," he said. "Where's the charger?"

"The charger?" Gertrude pinched her lips as she looked around her living room, all the while blocking the man's access to the front door. "I don't think I've seen that thing in years. My daughter might have thrown it in the trash. Don't think it was working."

The poor man's mouth opened and closed, but nothing came out.

"You don't look so good," Gertrude said and placed a hand on his shoulder. "Would you like a cup of coffee?"

The surprised look on his face bordered on comical. He frowned, making his eyebrows come down to a normal level.

"I don't—" He sputtered. "I don't want no bloody *cup* of *coffee*! I've had enough of the stuff already, thank you very much!" He waved at his over-sized t-shirt and bare legs.

He heaved himself into an upright position and took a step toward Gertrude. "How do you expect me to fix the phone if. Its. Battery's. Dead?" He punctuated his words by poking a finger into Gertrude's shoulder, making her step back against the front door.

"I thought you weren't here for the phone," Gertrude said, her own anger rising. "I thought you were here to install your Trojan horse and relieve me of all my money?"

"You're the one who—" The youngster cut off mid-sentence as Gertrude's words registered.

He took a step back. "What did you just say?"

Eying the computer, wondering if they were still in the camera's field of vision, Gertrude straightened her back. "You heard me, young man. You were going to do what you did to that poor couple and steal all my money just because I don't know computers as well as you do."

The boy's face went slack with surprise for a short moment—before folding into a grimace as he bent in half and his stomach gave a loud growl.

"Hmm," Gertrude said, her face neutral. "Sounds like an unhappy stomach. Maybe it's something you ate?"

He hissed in a breath. Lunged for Gertrude.

Or at least he tried to. It's not easy to lunge while bent in half.

Gertrude sidestepped the attack and placed herself smack in front of her computer. There was no point in running away, because even in his reduced state, the young man would be able to catch her in no time.

Indeed, seconds later, he was in her personal space, breathing heavily and eyes darting from her face, to the door, to the computer with its prancing Greek.

"What was in that pie?" he asked. "What did you do to your computer?"

"*I* didn't do anything to the computer," Gertrude said, voice shaking but standing her ground. "My granddaughter might have, though. You'd have to ask her."

The young man growled, and his stomach echoed the sound. "I'm not asking her," he ground out, drops of sweat popping out on his forehead. "I'm asking you." He grabbed hold of Gertrude's throat and pushed her into the cupboard behind her.

He didn't cut off her breathing, but Gertrude was having second thoughts about her prank. This was where Robert would have stepped in and saved her, his bulk a natural deterrent to little upstarts like this boy.

"I'll answer you," said a voice from the computer.

Eyes so big Gertrude worried they'd fall out, the youngster turned to look at the screen, his hand still on her throat.

"I'll answer you," Céline's voice repeated. "But you have to let my grandmother go."

The boy switched his gaze to Gertrude, incredulity marking his features.

"I installed a software that stops your Trojan horse from functioning," Céline said calmly. "And I've been recording since the moment you walked through the door. Now. I've already called the police. Unless you want them to come through the door weapons first, I suggest *you let my grandmother go.*"

Face red and lips pulled back in a snarl, the young man turned his back on the computer to face Gertrude. "You nasty old—"

A large growl sounded from his stomach. He bent in half, head-butting Gertrude in the chest in the process. Then there was an explosion at the other end.

When the police burst through the door five minutes later, Gertrude sat in front of her computer, chatting with her granddaughter on Skype, taking notes on her next "how to" tab, which she intended to put to use as soon as someone had cleaned up the mess in her living room.

THANK YOU

THANK YOU FOR reading *Gertrude and the Trojan Horse*. I hope you enjoyed it.

I certainly enjoyed writing it!

If you liked the story, you might want to check out some of my other books mentioned on the next page. It's mostly Mysteries, but a few other genres will pop up, too.

And don't forget that the first book of my *Tolosa Mystery* series, *The Red Brick Haze*, is available for free on my website.

R.W. Wallace
www.rwwallace.com

Also by R.W. Wallace

Mystery

The Tolosa Mystery Series
The Red Brick Haze (free)
The Red Brick Cellars
The Red Brick Basilica

Ghost Detective Shorts (coming soon)
Just Desserts
Lost Friends
Family Bonds
Till Death
Family History
Common Ground
Heritage
Eternal Bond
New Beginnings

Short Stories
Cold Blue Eternity
Hidden Horrors
Critters
Gertrude and the Trojan Horse
First Impressions
Let Them Eat Cake
Out of Sight
Two's Company
Like Mother Like Daughter

Fantasy (Short Stories)
Unexpected Consequences
Morbier Impossible
A Second Chance

Science Fiction (Short Stories)
The Vanguard

Lollapalooza Shorts
Quarantine
Common Enemies
Coiled Danger
Mars Meeting

Adventure (Short Stories)
Size Matters

ABOUT THE AUTHOR

R.W. WALLACE WRITES in most genres, though she tends to end up in mystery more often than not. Dead bodies keep popping up all over the place whenever she sits down in front of her keyboard.

The stories mostly take place in Norway or France; the country she was born in and the one that has been her home for two decades. Don't ask her why she writes in English—she won't have a sensible answer for you.

Her Ghost Detective short story series appears in *Pulphouse Magazine*, starting in issue #9.

You can find all her books, long and short, all genres, on rwwallace.com.

www.ingramcontent.com/pod-product-compliance
Lightning Source LLC
LaVergne TN
LVHW041602070526
838199LV00046B/2108